GUARDIANS OF THE GALAXY

MARVEL

GUARDIANS OF THE GALAXY

BASED ON THE TV SERIES WRITTEN BY

STEVEN MELCHING, MAIRGHREAD SCOTT, DAVID MCDERMOTT, MARSHA GRIFFIN & MARTY ISENBERG

DIRECTED BY

JAMES YANG & JEFF WAMESTER

ANIMATION ART PRODUCED BY

MARVEL ANIMATION STUDIOS

ADAPTED BY

JOE CARAMAGNA

SPECIAL THANKS TO

HANNAH MACDONALD & PRODUCT FACTORY

EDITOR

CHRISTINA HARRINGTON

SENIOR EDITOR

MARK PANICCIA

COLLECTION EDITOR: **JENNIFER GRÜNWALD**
ASSISTANT EDITOR: **CAITLIN O'CONNELL**
ASSOCIATE MANAGING EDITOR: **KATERI WOODY**
EDITOR, SPECIAL PROJECTS: **MARK D. BEAZLEY**
VP PRODUCTION & SPECIAL PROJECTS: **JEFF YOUNGQUIST**
SVP PRINT, SALES & MARKETING: **DAVID GABRIEL**
HEAD OF MARVEL TELEVISION: **JEPH LOEB**

EDITOR IN CHIEF: **C.B. CEBULSKI**
CHIEF CREATIVE OFFICER: **JOE QUESADA**
PRESIDENT: **DAN BUCKLEY**
EXECUTIVE PRODUCER: **ALAN FINE**

MARVEL UNIVERSE GUARDIANS OF THE GALAXY VOL. 6. Contains material originally published in magazine form as MARVEL UNIVERSE GUARDIANS OF THE GALAXY #20-23. First printing 2018. ISBN 978-1-302-90511-8. Published by MARVEL WORLDWIDE, INC., a subsidiary of MARVEL ENTERTAINMENT, LLC. OFFICE OF PUBLICATION: 135 West 50th Street, New York, NY 10020. Copyright © 2018 MARVEL No similarity between any of the names, characters, persons, and/or institutions in this magazine with those of any living or dead person or institution is intended, and any such similarity which may exist is purely coincidental. **Printed in the U.S.A.** DAN BUCKLEY, President, Marvel Entertainment; JOE QUESADA, Chief Creative Officer; TOM BREVOORT, SVP of Publishing; DAVID BOGART, SVP of Business Affairs & Operations, Publishing & Partnership; DAVID GABRIEL, SVP of Sales & Marketing, Publishing; JEFF YOUNGQUIST, VP of Production & Special Projects; DAN CARR, Executive Director of Publishing Technology; ALEX MORALES, Director of Publishing Operations; SUSAN CRESPI, Production Manager; STAN LEE, Chairman Emeritus. For information regarding advertising in Marvel Comics or on Marvel.com, please contact Vit DeBellis, Custom Solutions & Integrated Advertising Manager, at vdebellis@marvel.com. For Marvel subscription inquiries, please call 888-511-5480. **Manufactured between 12/15/2017 and 1/16/2018 by** SHERIDAN, CHELSEA, MI, USA.

9 8 7 6 5 4 3 2 1

GUARDIANS OF THE GALAXY

ROCKET

GROOT

DRAX THE DESTROYER

GAMORA

PETER QUILL, A.K.A. STAR-LORD

PREVIOUSLY:

The Guardians came into possession of a mysterious Spartaxan cube that holds a map to an object of immense power called the Cosmic Seed. The Guardians traveled to Spartax to find out why Star-Lord is the only one able to access the map, and discovered that he is actually the heir to King J'Son and the Spartax Empire! And unbeknownst to Star-Lord, J'Son has been manipulating him into finding the Cosmic Seed for Thanos!

HEAR ME, SPARTAX! THE SHADOW OF *THANOS* DARKENS YOUR WORLD--

--SUBMIT TO MY WILL OR *PERISH!*

ANGELA, HEIMDALL-- LET US SHOW THE MAD TITAN THE MIGHT OF ASGARD!

BRING IT ON, CHILDREN OF ASGARD.

HNN!

ZZRRSH!

BEGONE, THANOS--

--OR THIS DAY WILL SEE YOUR *RUIN* AND THIS WORLD SHALL BECOME YOUR *TOMB!*

FWASH!

FOOLS.

THANOS. NOW I CAN FINALLY HAVE REVENGE FOR HIS DESTRUCTION OF MY FAMILY!

GET IN LINE, DRAX!

WHERE IS THIS LINE, GAMORA? I WILL *FIGHT* MY WAY TO THE *FRONT*!

JUST LIGHT 'IM UP!

ZARK! ZARK! ZARK!

GUARDIANS OF THE GALAXY-- SURELY YOU DID NOT THINK YOU HAD SEEN THE *LAST* OF THANOS.

KRAKK!

RRRMMMBB

AFTER OUR PREVIOUS BATTLE, DO YOU REALLY BELIEVE THAT YOU STAND A CHANCE OF EXACTING REVENGE ON ME?

YOUR FRIENDS HAVE BEEN DEFEATED IN ONE FELL SWOOP. NOW THIS IS *YOUR* END, STAR-LORD.

AS A WISE EARTH-MAN ONCE SAID, "UP YOUR NOSE WITH A RUBBER HOSE."

LORD THANOS, WAIT! YOU MUST SPARE MY SON!

WHY SHOULD I DO SUCH A THING, J'SON?

"--OR YOU'LL FIND OUT WHAT REAL PAIN IS!"

NYAAH!

SHHRR!

WHERE IS THE COSMIC SEED, SPARTAXAN?

HALF-SPARTAXAN. AND YOU DIDN'T SAY *"PLEASE."*

SHHRR!

AAAAH!

HNN. I DON'T *KNOW* WHERE THE SEED IS.

I BELIEVE YOU, BUT YOUR *CRYPTO-CUBE* DOES KNOW WHERE TO FIND IT--

--AND *YOU'RE* THE ONLY ONE WHO CAN *OPEN* IT. IF YOU DON'T KNOW WHERE THE SEED IS--

--PROVE IT.

AND LET YOU POWER UP WITH THE RESIDUAL COSMIC SEED ENERGY INSIDE? *NO WAY!*

THEN PERHAPS IT'S TIME I TRIED *SOMETHING ELSE.*

SHHRR!

AAAAH!

I AM NEWT.

YOU BOTH SEEM SO... FAMILIAR.

YOU WERE BOTH IN MY DREAM. AND SO WAS MY FATHER...?

THE HIMALAYAS ARE HOME TO THE TALLEST MOUNTAINS ON EARTH--

CLK!

SORRY, LET ME SHUT THAT OFF FOR YOU.

HOW ARE YOU FEELING TODAY, MEREDITH?

G-GAMORA? DRAX?

YOU WERE IN MY DREAM, TOO! THIS IS SO WEIRD.

PETER! YOU'RE ALL OUT OF SORTS TODAY.

MAYBE THIS WILL MAKE YOU FEEL BETTER. I HAVE A GIFT FOR YOU.

THIS?

GO ON--

--OPEN IT.

NO. THIS ISN'T RIGHT. I FEEL LIKE I'M NOT *SUPPOSED* TO.

THIS-- THIS CAN'T BE *REAL.*

EEEEEEEE

WE'RE *LOSING* HER!

THE ONLY THING THAT CAN SAVE HER IS IN THAT *BOX!*

OPEN IT! *HURRY!*

EEEEEEEE

EEEEEEEE

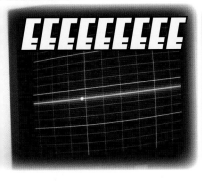

I--I CAN'T LOSE YOU *AGAIN,* MOM!

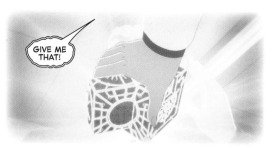

GIVE ME THAT!

W-WHAT?

HA HA HA HA HA!

YOU USED *MY OWN* MEMORIES *AGAINST* ME! THAT IS PURE *EVIL!*

THERE IS NO GOOD OR EVIL--THERE IS ONLY THE WILL OF *THANOS.*

AND WITH THE POWER OF THE COSMIC SEED, THANOS IS ALL-POWERFUL.

ACCORDING TO MY COMM LINK SIGNAL, WE SHOULD BE CLOSING IN ON THANOS' LOCATION.

J'SON'S ACTUALLY TELLING THE TRUTH--

--THERE'S A SENTRY SHIP DEAD AHEAD!

I'LL JAM HIS COMMUNICATIONS SO HE DOESN'T SEE US COMING, ROCKET.

THERE IS NO HONOR IN A *SNEAK ATTACK!*

I AM *GROOT!*

THERE MUST BE A *MILLION* FIGHTER SHIPS OUT THERE! ROCKET, ENGAGE OUR *CLOAKING* DEVICE--

DRAX IS RIGHT--LET THEM SEE US COMING!

SHRIPP!

KING *JERKFACE SABOTAGED* THE *CLOAK!*

HEH HEH. THE CUBE BELONGS TO THANOS ONCE MORE.

GET AWAY FROM IT!

KRKK!

FREEZING THIS DEVICE WILL NOT *DESTROY* IT, STAR-LORD.

NO...

...BUT IT'LL MAKE IT REALLLLY *BRITTLE* IN THOSE BIG MITTS OF YOURS!

BBKOOOM!

gnWW!

WH-WHAT'S HAPPENING?!

I'M *SEEING* THINGS!

UH-OH. I'D BETTER GET GOING WHILE I STILL--

J'SON OF SPARTAX!

YOU ARE UNDER ARREST FOR TREASON--

--SO SAYS YOUR DAUGHTER, **CAPTAIN VICTORIA**, COMMANDER OF THE SPARTAX ROYAL GUARD. AND, AS PER THE STAR-LORD'S REQUEST--

--ACTING **QUEEN OF SPARTAX!**

"THANOS DISAPPEARED IN THE BLAST, BUT IF THE PAST HAS TAUGHT US ANYTHING, IT'S THAT WE HAVE NOT SEEN THE **LAST** OF HIM."

WE MUST CONTINUE OUR SEARCH FOR THE COSMIC SEED TO ENSURE IT DOES NOT FALL INTO HIS HANDS.

WE KNOW YOU **STOLE** THE COSMIC SEED TO ORCHESTRATE THIS ASGARDIAN WAR WITH SPARTAX, LOKI...

IF YOU'D LIKE TO SAVE ANY SHRED OF DIGNITY YOU HAVE LEFT, YOU WILL TELL US WHERE IT IS.

I'M AFRAID I *CANNOT* TELL YOU, BROTHER.

YOU *WILL* TELL ME! *NOW!*

I MEAN, I *LITERALLY* CANNOT TELL YOU.

AFTER I STOLE THE COSMIC SEED BACK FROM J'SON, I USED MY TRICKSTER POWERS TO HIDE IT WHERE NO ONE COULD EVER FIND IT--

--INCLUDING *ME.*

WHY WOULD YOU DO SUCH A THING?

THE SEED CLEARLY WASN'T SAFE IN *ASGARD*, SO I DID THE GALAXY A *FAVOR.*

I'M A *HERO.*

I BEG TO DIFFER... BUT IF WHAT YOU SAY IS TRUE, THEN YOU ARE NOT A VILLAIN EITHER.

AND I HOPE YOU ARE RIGHT--

"--AND THAT THE COSMIC SEED IS LOST *FOREVER*."

ROCKET, TAKE THE CONTROLS. I'M NOT FEELING SO WELL.

MY BOND TO THE CRYPTO-CUBE MUST'VE BEEN STRONGER THAN I THOUGHT. ITS DESTRUCTION TOOK A LOT OUT OF ME.

"I THINK I NEED A NAP."

NO WAY!

THOSE IMAGES-- I KNOW HOW TO FIND THE COSMIC SEED!

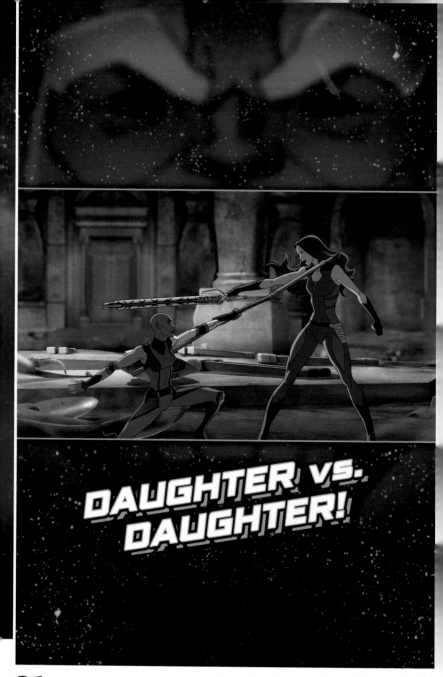

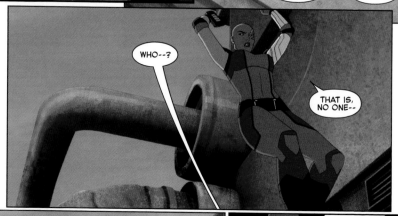

HNN. WH-WHERE AM I?

BINDERS?

WELL, WE WEREN'T SIMPLY GOING TO LET YOU WALK OUT OF HERE.

RONAN! WHATEVER YOU HAVE PLANNED FOR ME, GET IT OVER WITH!

I DON'T WANT TO LISTEN TO YOUR SPEECHES ANY LONGER THAN I HAVE TO.

VERY WELL.

GAMORA, YOU ARE ACCUSED OF BETRAYING MY SACRED MISSION AND OTHER CRIMES AGAINST THE GALAXY.

BUT I'M NOT GOING TO SIMPLY END YOU--I'M GOING TO MAKE AN EXAMPLE OF YOU.

AND THAT'S WHERE I COME IN.

THE GRAND-MASTER?!

I'M ON CONJUNCTION?

YES. AND I HAVE SOMETHING VERY SPECIAL PLANNED FOR YOU AND FOR OUR VIEWING AUDIENCE ACROSS THE GALAXY--

"--AN EXECUTION WITH *FLAIR!*"

LADIES AND GENTLEMEN, WELCOME TO THE *CONJUNCTION ARENA* FOR A *SPECIAL PRESENTATION*--

--THE *TRIAL BY COMBAT* OF THANOS' DAUGHTER *GAMORA!*

THIS IS WHAT I GET FOR TRYING TO RIGHT A WRONG.

AT LEAST YOU'RE TAKING OFF THESE BINDERS SO I HAVE A FIGHTING CHANCE--

CLINK!

--NOW GIVE ME MY *SWORD!*

YOU DIDN'T THINK I'D GIVE YOU AN *ADVANTAGE*, DO YOU? WHAT KIND OF AN *EXECUTIONER* WOULD THAT MAKE ME?

THE RULES ARE *SIMPLE*--

NO!

COME ON-- OPEN UP AND *DRAIN* THIS TUB BEFORE THE WATER RISES TOO HIGH!

IT IS NO USE!

TURN AND *FIGHT* ME, GAMORA! YOU WILL *PAY* FOR WHAT YOU HAVE DONE!

YOU?!

LADIES AND GENTLEMEN, GAMORA'S NEXT OPPONENT-- *JARHEAD!*

HOW DID HE END UP AS A BRAIN IN A JAR? LET'S JUST SAY HE BLAMES GAMORA!

AND IF SHE WISHES TO GET OUT ALIVE, SHE MUST HURRY--JARHEAD HAS THE *ONLY KEY* TO THE DRAIN AND HE DOESN'T LOOK WILLING TO SHARE!

PIECE OF CAKE.

DO YOU THINK SO? GRANDMASTER LEFT OUT ONE IMPORTANT DETAIL--

--MY NEW *BODY* UPGRADE!

CRUD.

AND FOR OUR *FINAL* CHALLENGER, I PRESENT TO YOU THE SCOURGE OF THE GALAXY--

--THE ELEMENTAL *BEAST!*

HA! THAT LITTLE THING?

OKAY, SO HE CAN LIGHT HIMSELF ON *FIRE.* NOTED.

QUILL--

I'VE GOT THIS, GAMORA.

HERE'S *MUD* IN YOUR EYE, UGLY!

FOOSH!

SPLURCH!

SPLATCH!

FIRE'S OUT! ANYTHING ELSE YOU NEED ME TO DO?

IT'S AN *ELEMENTAL,* QUILL! YOU DIDN'T *DEFEAT* IT, YOU JUST CHANGED ITS PHYSICAL PROPERTIES!

SO WHAT HAPPENS WHEN WE BLAST IT WITH WIND?

WIND? THAT'S... BRILLIANT.

WELL, IT'S NOT ME WHO'S DOING IT!

HM. I SHOULD'VE KNOWN.

"I MUST RETURN IT TO HER."

ANTI-GRAVITY, ELEMENTAL COMBAT AND THE PRINCE OF SPARTAX? LADIES AND GENTLEMEN, THIS IS A RARE TREAT!

FROOSH!

I HAVE A *PLAN!*

I DON'T NEED YOU TO SHOOT MORE *MUD,* QUILL!

YES, THERE'S MUD...

SPLORCH!

KRKK!

...BUT IT'S IMMEDIATELY FOLLOWED BY *ICE!*

AND NOW OUR ELEMENTAL FRIEND IS NOTHING MORE THAN A PIÑATA!

AND THAT'S ALL, FOLKS! GAMORA'S OPPONENTS HAVE ALL BEEN DEFEATED, THANKS TO THE PRINCE OF SPARTAX!

NO NEED TO *THANK* ME, GAMORA.

YOU RUINED EVERYTHING, QUILL!

ABOUT MAKING UP FOR ALL THE THINGS I DID BACK WHEN I WAS WORKING FOR RONAN.

THIS ISN'T ABOUT *YOU*... IT WAS SUPPOSED TO BE ABOUT *ME*!

SO YOU'VE DONE BAD THINGS. I HAVE, TOO-- AS ONE OF YONDU'S *RAVAGERS*. THIS ISN'T MAKING *AMENDS*, THIS IS *PUNISHING* YOURSELF.

I WON'T STAND BY AND WATCH YOU DO THAT--

ACTION *AND* DRAMA? THIS WILL BE MY MOST MEMORABLE BROADCAST YET!

TO THINK WE HAVEN'T EVEN GOTTEN TO OUR MAIN EVENT YET-- GAMORA'S FINAL JUDGMENT...AND *EXECUTION*!

GAMORA! I HAVE FOUND YOUR *GRAVITY MATRIX*!

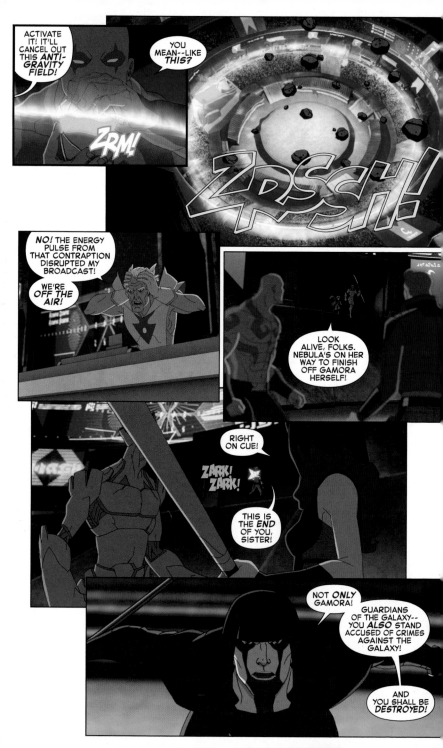

BASED ON "INHUMAN TOUCH" **22**

ATTILAN. HOME CITY OF THE INHUMANS.

I KNOW IT SOUNDS CRAZY, YOUR HIGHNESS, BUT...I'VE BEEN HAVING *VISIONS*--LIKE THE COSMIC SEED IS *TALKING* TO ME.

I THINK I KNOW WHERE IT IS, BUT I'VE GOT TO BE *SURE*...

I NEED TO TALK TO YOUR *BROTHER.*

BUT THAT'S--THAT'S *IMPOSSIBLE!*

MAXIMUS IS IN PRISON. IF WE RELEASE HIM OF THE MIND CONTROL, HE--

QUEEN MEDUSA, HE MAY BE MY LAST HOPE TO FIND THE COSMIC SEED.

IF THE ANSWER IS NO, I WANT TO HEAR IT FROM *BLACK BOLT* HIMSELF.

NOW YOU'RE *REALLY* ASKING FOR THE IMPOSSIBLE.

YOU KNOW BLACK BOLT'S VOICE IS DEADLY. IF HE EVEN UTTERS ONE *SYLLABLE*, WE'RE ALL *BLASTED* TO BITS!

NO ONE'S EVER THOUGHT OF THIS BEFORE? SERIOUSLY?

OKAY, YOUR HIGHNESS-- WHAT WILL IT BE?

AND I'D LIKE TO REMIND YOU THAT WE JUST SAVED YOUR ENTIRE KINGDOM FROM A PLAGUE.*

*SEE ISSUE #12 --HER HIGHNESS CHRISTINA

LATER...

THANKS FOR THIS. I REALLY--

YOU WILL HAVE EXACTLY *FIVE MINUTES* WITH HIM.

THERE IS *NO PHYSICAL CONTACT* ALLOWED.

YOU WILL NOT GIVE ANYTHING TO, NOR SHALL YOU ACCEPT ANYTHING FROM, THE PRISONER.

IS THAT CLEAR?

AS *CRYSTAL.*

STAR-LORD. I *KNEW* YOU'D RETURN.

YOU *DID?*

OF COURSE. I KNOW WHY YOU'RE HERE, AND I HAVE THE ANSWERS YOU SEEK.

BUT...

...THE INFORMATION IS FOR *STAR-LORD'S* EARS ONLY.

MEDUSA, DO YOU MIND?

IT'LL BE FINE.

FIVE MINUTES.

WHO NEEDS AN ENERGY AX WHEN I CAN USE *BRUTE FORCE?*

HUAHH!

MAXIMUS IS CONTROLLING THEM WITH HIS BRAIN HELMET AND IT'S TOTALLY *NOT* MY FAULT.

WHAM!

OKAY, IT'S MAYBE JUST A *LITTLE* MY FAULT.

WHY AM I NOT SURPRISED?

"JUST A QUICK STOP IN ATTILAN FOR A CHAT," HE SAID.

YEAH, I *KNOW* GORGON'S NOT IN THE MOOD FOR A CHAT--

I AM GROOT!

ZARK!

THE MIND-CONTROL SIGNAL IS COMIN' FROM THAT *TOWER!*

KEEP THE INHUMANS BUSY WHILE ME AN' GROOT *DISABLE* IT!

NO, *YOU* KEEP THEM BUSY, ROCKET, WHILE DRAX AND I GET THE *MIND-CONTROL HELMET* OFF OF *MAXIMUS!*

BUT IF *YOU* GUYS ARE GOING *THERE,* AND *YOU* GUYS ARE GOING *THERE,* ¿GULP¿ THEN--

I AM GROOT?

ALL I GOTTA DO IS GO UP THERE AND SHORT OUT THE POWER.

HMM. LET'S SEE HERE...

THIS OUGHT TO DO IT!

KRKK!

OH, *LOCKJAW!* YOU'RE ALL RIGHT!

I'M OKAY, TOO...

...IN CASE YOU WERE WONDERING.

MAXIMUS IS NO LONGER IN HIS CELL. WE BARELY MADE IT OUT BEFORE HE DESTROYED THE BUILDING.

THEN WHERE IS HE?

HEAR ME, INHUMANS--THE TIME HAS COME TO MAKE SOME CHANGES!

HE'S IN THE *PALACE!*

I-- *MAXIMUS THE MAGNIFICENT*--HAVE REPURPOSED THE ATTILAN DEFENSE SYSTEM USING THE POWER OF *TERRIGEN CRYSTALS* NOT FOR EVOLUTION, BUT FOR *REVOLUTION!*

KARNAK, HAVE YOU FOUND THE WEAK SPOT?

I CAN'T QUITE REACH IT. I NEED SOME MORE SLACK...

I...

...AM--

--GROOT!

SHRIPPP!

I AM GROOT!

AAHHH!

SLISSH!

HOW IS THAT FOR MORE SLACK?

"MAXIMUS!"

YOUR TOYS ARE NO MATCH FOR DRAX THE DESTROYER!

KING BLACK BOLT!

PLEASE, BROTHER--DON'T DESTROY THIS CONSOLE!

IF YOU DO, YOU'LL SHUT DOWN MY BEAUTIFUL CANNON!

ZRASH!

THIRTY--

--TWENTY-NINE--

--TWENTY-EIGHT--

HA HA! YOU JUST LOCKED THE TERRIGEN CANNON TO FIRE IN **30** SECONDS!

BECAUSE YOU DESTROYED THE CONSOLE, IT'S IMPOSSIBLE TO SHUT THE CANNON DOWN!

GOODBYE, BROTHER!

HE'S ESCAPING THROUGH THE **TRAP** DOOR!

--THREE--

--TWO--

MEDUSA, PULL US OUT! QUICK! BEFORE IT--

--ONE--

KAPOW!

WHEW! WE MADE IT OUT! BY A *HAIR*, AS THEY SAY!

BUT WHAT ABOL *MAXIMUS*

MAXIMUS ESCAPED THROUGH A *TRAP DOOR.*

WITH ALL OF THE CAVERNS BENEATH ATTILAN, HE COULD BE ANYWHERE.

VRRRRRRR!

HEY! THAT'S *MY* SHIP!

MAXIMUS IS STEALING THE *MILANO!*

...

BLACK BOLT...?

WHAT?

"--THROUGH SOME SMUGGLING COMPARTMENTS."

DO YOU THINK I'D LET YOU SAVE *MY* SHIP *WITHOUT* ME?

BESIDES, I KNOW THE WAY IN--

SNEAKING UP ON ME? WELL, YOU'RE *TOO LATE!*

WE'RE ALREADY HEADED STRAIGHT FOR ATTILAN'S *MAIN REACTORS!*

WHATEVER YOU DO, DON'T HIT THE SHIP'S *SELF-DESTRUCT* BUTTON!

IT'LL BLOW UP THE SHIP, ATTILAN-- *EVERYTHING* IN THIS SECTOR!

IT'S THAT BIG, SQUARE ONE ON THE END!

YOU MEAN *THIS* ONE?

CLIK!

GUARDIANS OF THE ...EARTH?!

GUEST-STARRING
EVERYONE'S FAVORITE TALKING DOG—
COSMO!

BASED ON "WELCOME BACK," "I'VE BEEN SEARCHING SO LONG"
& "I FEEL THE EARTH MOVE"

WE HAD TO GET OUT OF THERE--AND FAST! SO...

GET BACK HERE!

VVVRRRRRRRR

COSMO FORGET HOW MUCH HE LOVE WIND ON FACE--BUT PETER QUILL'S DRIVING NEED MUCH IMPROVEMENT.

CUT ME COME SLACK--I LEFT EARTH LONG BEFORE I WAS OLD ENOUGH TO DRIVE--

OH NO, IT'S KORATH! HE'S FOLLOWING US!

HOLD ON TO YOUR TAIL!

SKREET!

FWRMM!

GAH!

THAT SHOULD STUN KORATH FOR A WHILE. WHAT DO YOU SAY WE TAKE THIS SET OF WHEELS TO THE OLD *QUILL HOUSE?*

WE USED TO HAVE A *STORM CELLAR--* I BET MY DAD HID THE COSMIC SEED THERE.

YOU! OUT OF THE CAR!

NOT *YOU* AGAIN!

STAY BACK AND PUT YOUR HANDS IN THE AIR!

LOOK, COOGAN, I JUST--

I SAID TO STAY BACK!

SHUNK

SHUNK

ZZZZRRRKK!

D-D-D--

THE NEXT THING I REMEMBER, I WAS IN *JAIL*

LOOK, JUST GIVE ME A TICKET FOR WALKING MY DOG WITHOUT A LEASH AND LET ME OUT OF HERE.

YOU ALSO *STOLE A CAR.* BUT THAT'S NOT IMPORTANT RIGHT NOW.

YOU SAID THE NAME *"PETER QUILL."* WHAT DO YOU KNOW ABOUT HIM?

REALLY? *THAT'S* WHAT THIS IS ABOUT?

IT'S *PERSONAL,* OKAY? I--I USED TO *BULLY* HIM.

I FOUND OUT LATER THAT HIS MOM WAS REAL SICK. I WANTED TO APOLOGIZE, BUT HE DISAPPEARED.

THE GUILT'S BEEN HAUNTING ME FOR *YEARS.*

≥SIGH≤

I'M PETER QUILL.

I WAS ABDUCTED BY ALIENS AS A KID, FOUND OUT I WAS *SPACE ROYALTY,* AND NOW I'VE COME BACK TO EARTH TO FIND A SEED THAT GRANTS *UNLIMITED POWER.*

HA HA HA HA!

THAT'S THE MOST RIDICULOUS--

KRKKK!

SHRAMM!

YAAH!

PETER QUILL! YOU CANNOT ELUDE KORATH FOREVER!

HE CALLED YOU "QUILL." YOU MEAN YOU WERE TELLING THE *TRUTH?*

SHOW ME THE WAY TO THE COSMIC-- AAAH!

KROOM!

SOMEBODY NEED BAILIN' OUT?

YOUR MANGY MUTT, COSMO, TOLD US YOU GOT YOURSELF INTO TROUBLE ON THIS BACKWATER DIRT BALL OF A PLANET.

WE WERE *SHOCKED*, I TELL YA.

THAT WAS *SARCASM.*

AFTER WE CALMED COOGAN DOWN AND INTRODUCTIONS WERE MADE...

I WAS WRONG ABOUT THIS PLANET--IT'S NOT WORTHLESS AFTER ALL! THIS *"DUCT TAPE"* IS *AMAZING!*

IS *EVERYTHING* ON EARTH LIKE THIS?

WE'LL SHOP *LATER*, ROCKET. FIRST, WE HAVE TO FIND THE COSMIC SEED.

HOLD UP, PETER. I'M COMING WITH YOU.

THAT'S NOT A GOOD IDEA--THIS COULD GET *DANGEROUS.*

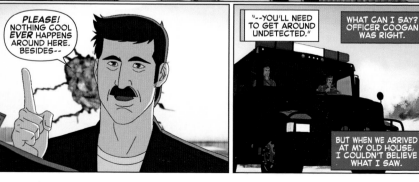

PLEASE! NOTHING COOL *EVER* HAPPENS AROUND HERE. BESIDES--

"--YOU'LL NEED TO GET AROUND UNDETECTED."

WHAT CAN I SAY? OFFICER COOGAN WAS RIGHT.

BUT WHEN WE ARRIVED AT MY OLD HOUSE, I COULDN'T BELIEVE WHAT I SAW.

QUILL, YOUR HOUSE IS VERY LARGE.

ARE ALL OF THESE CARS *YOURS?*

THIS ISN'T MY HOUSE, GAMORA--

--IT'S A *MALL!*

SORRY, PETER, I SHOULD'VE TOLD YOU SOONER--THEY BUILT IT SHORTLY AFTER YOU LEFT.

BUT I'M SURE THE STORM CELLAR IS STILL *UNDERNEATH* IT *SOMEWHERE--*

"--WE'LL JUST HAVE TO LOOK AROUND FOR A BIT."

SEE? YOU'RE BLENDING RIGHT IN.

RIGHT...

SURE ENOUGH, COOGAN WAS RIGHT! I DON'T KNOW *HOW*, BUT *SOMETHING* WAS TELLING ME I WAS STANDING RIGHT *OVER* THE CELLAR.

GUYS! THIS IS IT!

OOH! ONE OF THESE THINGS HOLDS *10,000 SONGS?*

AS IT TURNS OUT, THERE WAS AN EMERGENCY HATCH UNDER THE KIOSK.

THE CELLAR WAS EMPTY, BUT JUST AS I REMEMBERED IT.

THEN...

COOGAN, I'VE FOUND SOMETHING!

YOU MIGHT WANT TO STAND BACK. THE COSMIC SEED IS VERY POWERFUL...AND *UNPREDICTABLE.*

HUH?! MY OLD COMIC BOOK COLLECTION?!

BRMMB!

WHAT IS THAT?

DID YOU THINK RONAN SENT ME AFTER YOU *ALONE?* MY ARMY FREED ME FROM YOUR WEAK EARTH MATERIALS.

HEY! WATCH WHAT YOU SAY ABOUT *DUCT TAPE!*

QUILL, GRAB THE SEED AND LET'S GET OUT OF HERE!

SUSH!!

YEAH... ABOUT THE SEED, GAMORA...

DON'T TELL ME THIS WAS *ANOTHER* WILD GOOSE CHASE--

ZRRT!

KRUTACK! THEIR SHOTS CAUSED A POWER SURGE IN MY ADJUSTABLE IMPLOSIVE DEVICE!

IT SET A COUNTDOWN! IN TEN SECONDS THIS ENTIRE MALL--AND EVERYTHING IN IT--WILL SHRINK DOWN TO THE SIZE OF MY FIST.

AND I HAVE *TINY HANDS!*

AND NEITHER DID COOGAN.

AAAAH!

WHAT HAPPENED?

WE TELEPORTED TO A PLACE CALLED KNOWHERE, THEN TELEPORTED BACK.

YOU MEAN...THIS IS THE MALL?

NO...

...*THIS* IS THE MALL. IN THIS BOX.

DON'T WORRY, I'M SURE I'LL FIGURE OUT HOW TO GET THE INNOCENT BYSTANDERS OUT AND BACK TO NORMAL.

THANKS FOR LETTING ME TAG ALONG ON YOUR ADVENTURE, PETER.

I'M SORRY FOR ALL THAT I PUT YOU THROUGH WHEN YOU WERE A KID, I--

YOU WERE JUST A KID YOURSELF. IT'S WATER UNDER THE BRIDGE.

AND I MEANT IT. I SPENT MOST OF MY LIFE HATING A PLANET FOR THINGS THAT HAPPENED A LONG TIME AGO...

...AND IT WAS TIME TO LEAVE IT ALL BEHIND.

BUT IF I WEREN'T *HATING* EARTH FROM LIGHT-YEARS AWAY...

...AND THERE WAS NOTHING THERE FOR ME TO *LOVE*, EITHER...

...WOULD I EVENTUALLY *FORGET* ABOUT IT FOREVER?

QUILL, DID YOU HEAR WHAT I SAID?

I AM GROOT?

I SAID MAYBE THIS IS *GOOD* NEWS. MAYBE IT MEANS THE SEED IS LOST FOREVER.

BUT WHAT IF IT *ISN'T?* MAXIMUS CONFIRMED THAT IT WAS ON EARTH--

WAIT A SECOND.

WE KNOW THE COSMIC SEED LEFT TRACES OF ENERGY EVERYWHERE IT WENT. ONE OF THOSE PLACES WAS *ATTILAN*, HOME OF THE INHUMANS.

WE DIDN'T FIND THE SEED IN ATTILAN, OBVIOUSLY, BUT ATTILAN *USED* TO BE ON *EARTH.*

WHAT IF THE SEED ISN'T WHERE MY *HOUSE* USED TO BE, BUT WHERE *ATTILAN* USED TO BE!

YOU DON'T MEAN--

"YUP! WE'RE GOING *BACK* TO EARTH!"

WHAT IS THIS PLACE, QUILL? I KNEW I SHOULD'VE TELEPORTED BACK TO KNOWHERE WITH COSMO.

EW! WHAT IS THIS SURFACE?

IT'S STICKY! LIKE... LIKE...

SKREEEEE!

...A WEB!

MEANWHILE...

FOOTPRINTS! THE GUARDIANS ARE IN THERE, MY LORD.

THEN COME, NEBULA. THE FOOLS WILL LEAD US RIGHT TO THE SEED--AND ULTIMATE POWER!

WE WALKED FOR WHAT FELT LIKE HOURS, UNTIL FINALLY...

UP *THERE!* IN THAT *BOX!* I THINK WE'VE FOUND IT!

INDEED YOU HAVE, STAR-LORD.

AND *YOU* LED *ME* RIGHT TO IT.

RONAN!

FEAR NOT, GUARDIANS. TO THANK YOU FOR YOUR *GENEROSITY,* I WILL ALLOW YOU ALL TO *LIVE.*

NO...

AH, THE COSMIC SEED...

...IT IS AS *MAGNIFICENT* AS I HAD IMAGINED.

WE WON'T LET YOU *LEAVE* HERE WITH IT, RONAN!

I'M AFRAID, GAMORA...

...YOU DO NOT HAVE A *CHOICE!*

KRAKK!

SHROOM!

"...AND GET RID OF THEM!"

I AM...

...GROOT!

NEBULA'S NEW STRENGTH IS *NOTHING* COMPARED TO *THAT* OF DRAX THE *DESTROYER!*

NO, DRAX! LET *GROOT* DEAL WITH MY SISTER. WE HAVE TO KEEP CLIMBING!

"WE CAN'T LET RONAN GET AWAY IN HIS SHIP!"

BUT THE COSMIC SEED MADE RONAN *TOO STRONG.* NONE OF OUR WEAPONS COULD DEFEAT HIM...

...EXCEPT FOR *ONE!*

WHAP!

HOW'S MY EARTHER *DUCT TAPE* TASTE, KRUTACKER?

SHREEP!

MMMF!

HOLD HIM STILL!

THE BOX'S RESIDUAL ENERGY IS PULLING THE COSMIC SEED OUT OF RONAN'S WEAPON!

GOT IT! *ER, WHAT IS THAT?*

FOOL! RONAN'S COSMIC POWER IS WANING! THE STALK IS SHRINKING!

RMMMM!

I AM GROOT!

GROOT, YOU'RE A GENIUS!

EVERYONE GRAB ON TO THE *GROOT-CHUTE!*

RMMMM!

CRASH!

THE END!